Happiness Is...

Marcus Pfister

NorthSouth

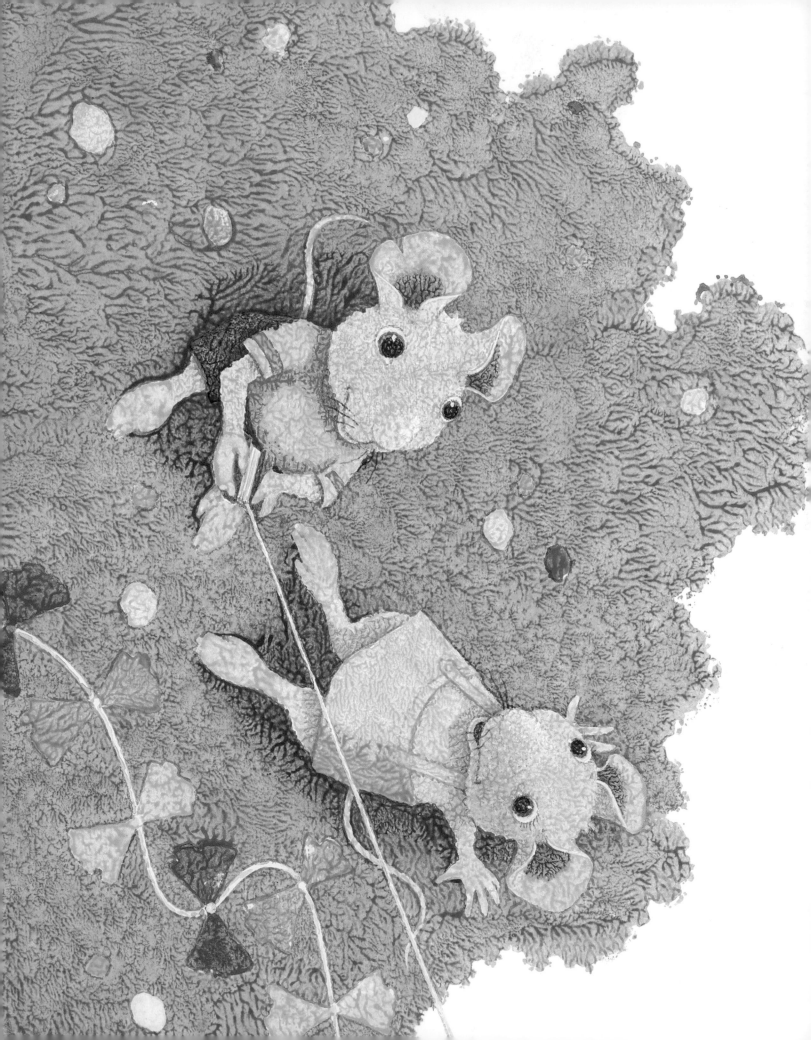

Zoe was sitting in the meadow lost in thought. The kite Leo was flying filled her with delight.

"Do you know what happiness is?" Zoe asked her best mouse-friend.

"Hmmm . . . ," answered Leo, tugging at the kite's string. "Is it that important?"

"Happiness is the most important thing of all," Zoe replied.

"Happiness is feeling a snowflake melt on your tongue in the winter."

Leo looked at her doubtfully.

"Happiness is finding the most beautiful pebble in the world.

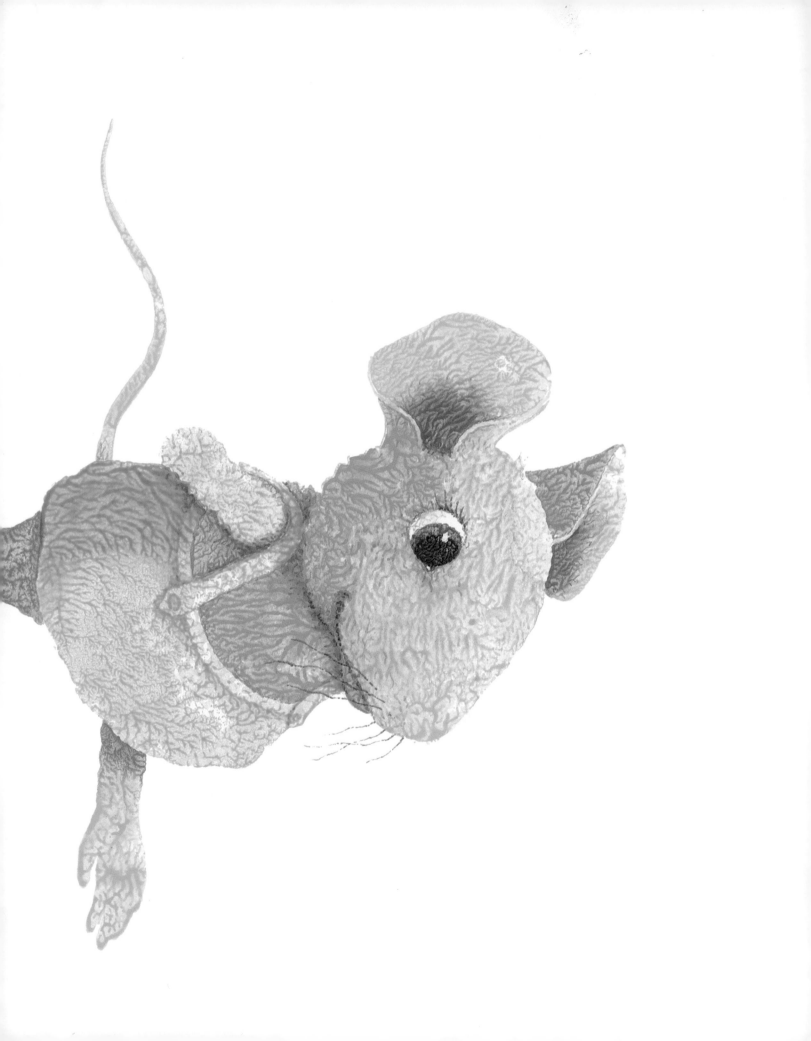

"And happiness is watching the course of a downy feather's flight."

"Hmm, I get it," Leo said gruffly.
"Happiness is discovering a little piece of
cheese deep in your trouser pocket."

"Happiness is blowing the seeds of a dandelion!" shouted Zoe.

"Happiness is jumping into a great big puddle!" declared Leo excitedly.

"Happiness is being kissed on the nose by a warm sunbeam," said Zoe.

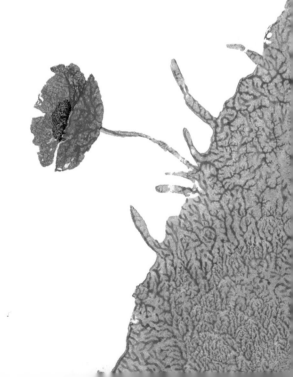

"Happiness is shuffling through a thick carpet of autumn leaves," exclaimed Leo.

Zoe lay down again in the grass and looked
up at the kite as it climbed higher and higher.
Then she turned over onto her tummy.

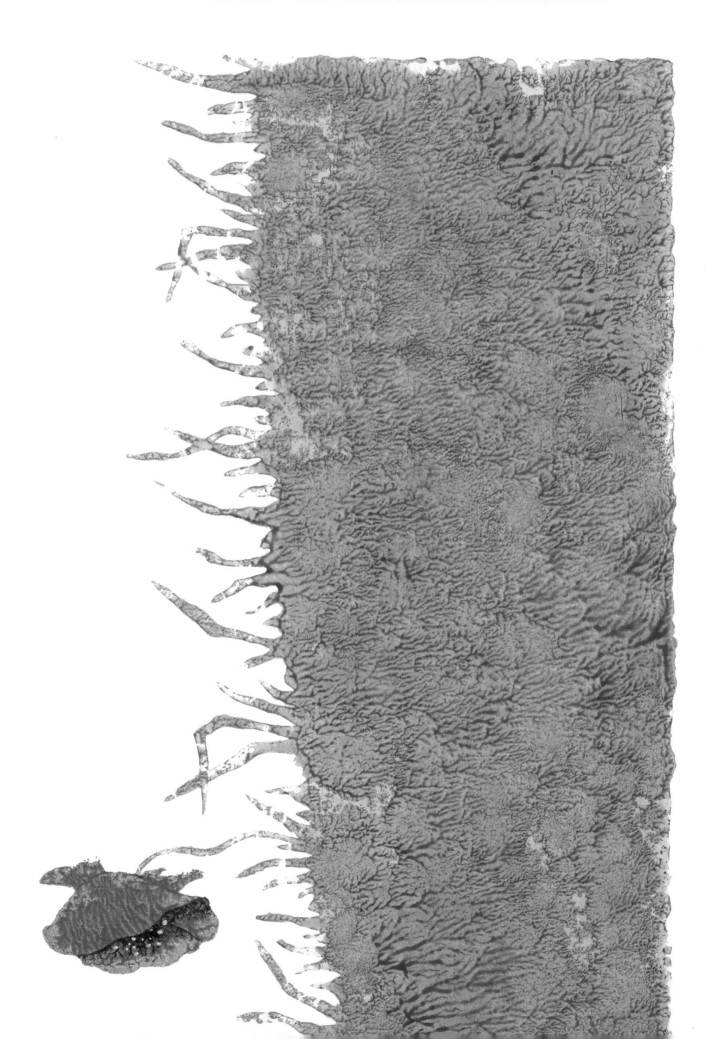

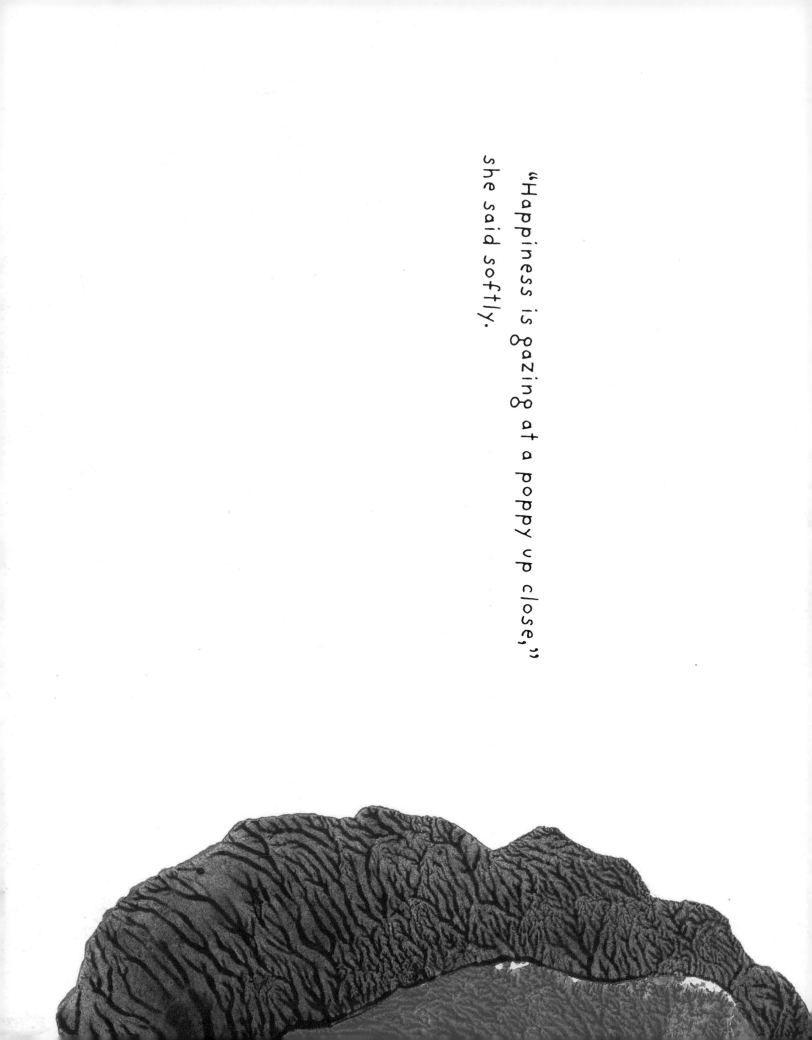

"Happiness is gazing at a poppy up close," she said softly.

"And happiness is flying a kite with your best friend!" said Leo with a shout of joy.

"Exactly. That's exactly what happiness is," Zoe said, and off they ran through the meadow together.

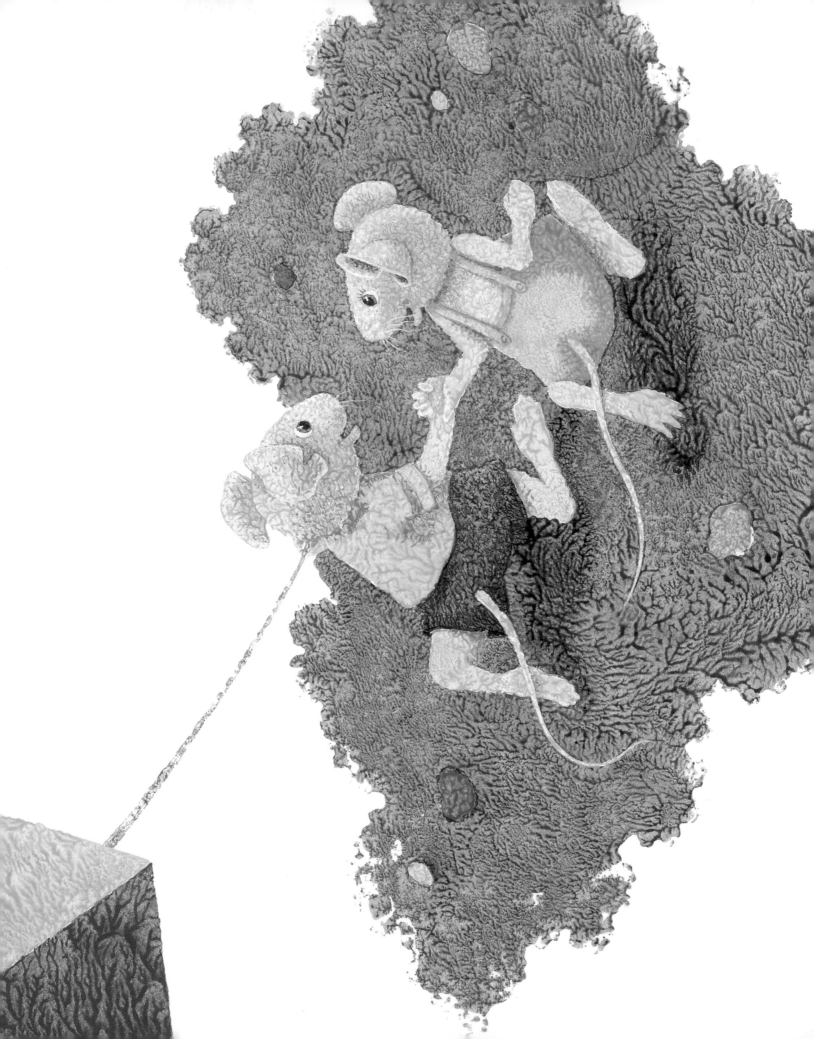